About the Book

Her father says, "How could an alligator get under your bed, Jill?"
Her mother says, "Go to sleep, dear," and returns to the guests in
the living room. But Jill can't sleep, and no matter how tightly she
hugs the blankets around her and puts the covers over her ears, she
can still hear that alligator snorting happily in the dark. Finally
Jill yells, "Help!" And Uncle Harry, who knows all about imagi-
native and not-so-very sleepy girls, comes to the rescue.

Joan Lowery Nixon has written a perceptive and funny story
about a comical trio—wide-awake Jill, fat, loving Uncle Harry,
and a chomping alligator named Alberta . . . all beautifully drawn
in bright colors by Jan Hughes.

THE ALLIGATOR UNDER THE BED

by Joan Lowery Nixon   illustrated by Jan Hughes

G. P. Putnam's Sons · New York

Text Copyright © 1974 by Joan Lowery Nixon
Illustrations Copyright © 1974 by Jan Hughes
All rights reserved.
Published simultaneously in Canada by
Longman Canada Limited, Toronto.
SBN: GB 399-60914-8
SBN: TR 399-20423-7
Library of Congress Catalog Card Number: 72-94263
PRINTED IN THE UNITED STATES OF AMERICA
04207

With love to my parents,
Joseph and Margaret Lowery

Jill was sure there was an alligator under her bed.

It made swishing noises with its tail like an alligator.

It made a funny, rumbling laugh in its throat like an alligator.

"Mama!" Jill called. "Mama, come here!"

Her mother hurried into her room. "It's past your bedtime," she said. "I thought you would be asleep."

Jill hugged the blanket to her chin. "There's an alligator under my bed," she whispered.

"Now, now, Jill," she said. "You just had a dream. Go to sleep, dear."

She walked out of the bedroom and back to the living room, where the grown-ups were laughing and talking.

The alligator snorted happily, and Jill could hear his sharp teeth click together.

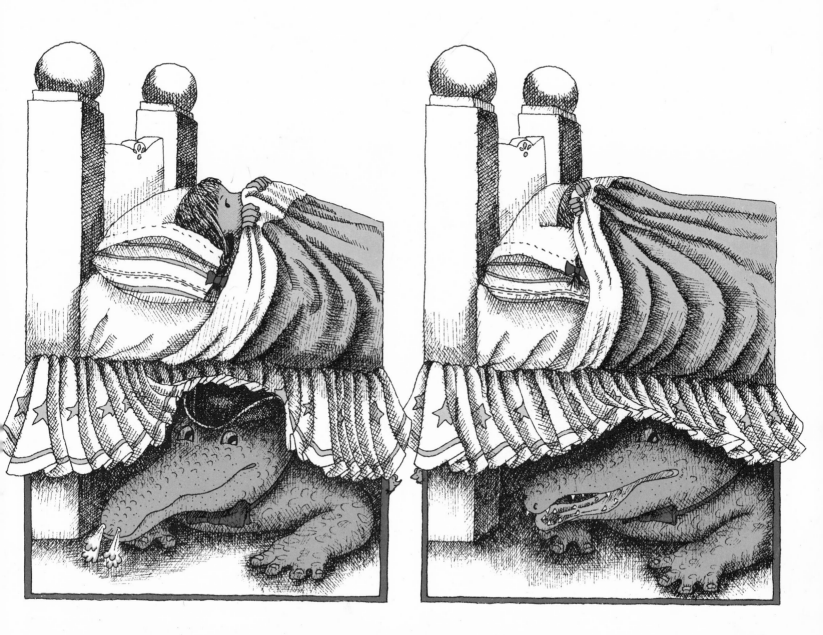

"Daddy!" she called. "I need you!"

Her father came into the room. "What's the matter? Can't sleep?" he asked.

Jill pulled the blanket up to her nose. "I can't sleep because there's a big alligator hiding under my bed!" she whispered.

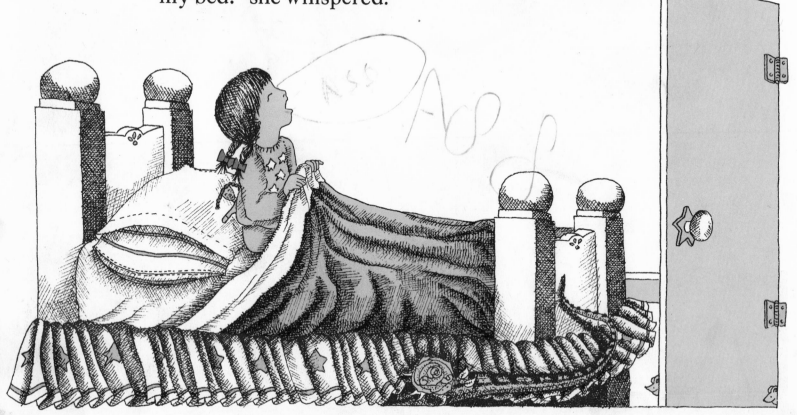

"Now, now," her father said. "Don't imagine things, Jill. How could an alligator get under your bed?"

He bent to give her a kiss and went back to the living room.

The alligator gurgled cheerfully and practiced chomping his big jaws together.

Jill kept quiet as long as she could. Then she shouted, "Help! There's an alligator under my bed!"

She heard footsteps coming down the hall. Uncle Harry stood in the doorway to her bedroom. He smiled and rubbed his double chins.

"I heard strange noises coming from this room," he said.

Jill peeked out from the top of the blanket. "It's the alligator," she whispered.

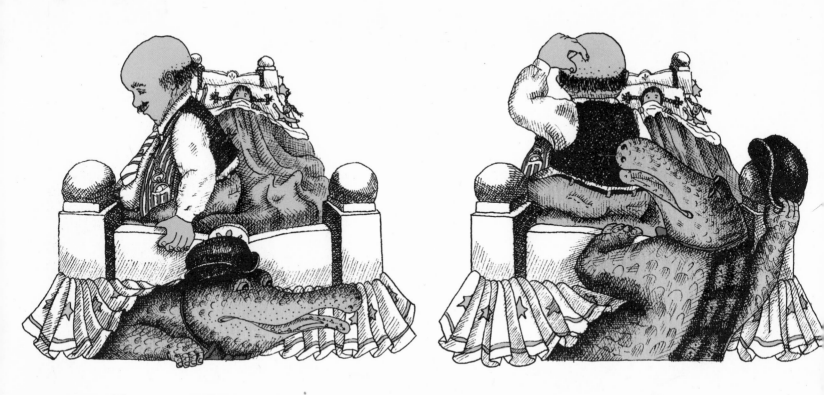

Uncle Harry sat on the bed next to Jill. "So that's where he is," he sighed.

"Who?" Jill asked.

"The alligator. His name is George, isn't it?"

"No," Jill said. "I think his name is Alberta."

Uncle Harry scratched his bald head. "I never was any good remembering names."

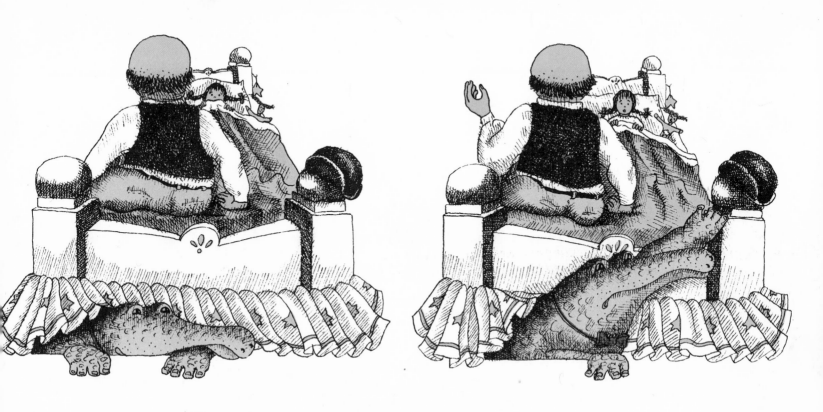

"Why is he under my bed?" Jill asked.

"He thinks it makes a good hiding place," Uncle Harry said. "It's a good thing you found him."

"Why?" Jill asked. She pulled the blanket down to her chin.

"Because when somebody loses a valuable thing like an alligator, naturally he wants him back."

Jill sat up in bed. "Who lost him?"

Uncle Harry shook his head sadly. "His wife and children. Isn't it a pity that he's here, hiding under your bed, when he should be home reading bedtime stories to his children?"

Jill thought a moment. "We better tell him to go home," she said.

"That's a good idea," Uncle Harry said. "You tell him because it's your bed he's under."

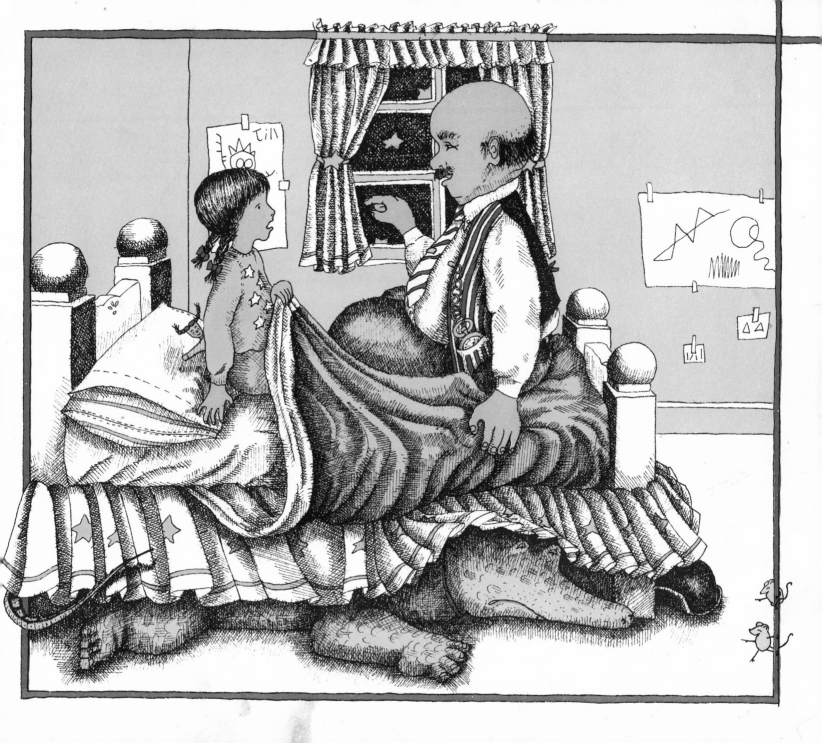

Jill leaned over and peered under the bed. It was dark there and very hard to see the alligator. But she shouted, "Go home, Alberta! Your wife wants you to go home right this minute!"

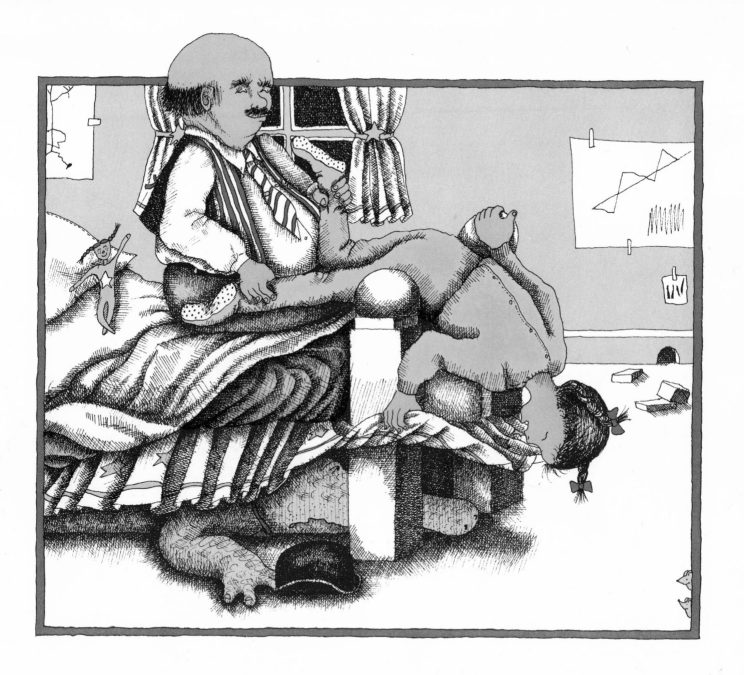

She sat up and looked at Uncle Harry.
"He wants to stay under the bed," she said.

Uncle Harry stood up. "The trouble with
alligators is that they are very proud. They don't
like you to know they can't do something. Alberta
is embarrassed to tell you that he doesn't know
how to open the front door."
"You could do it for him," Jill said.

"Good idea," Uncle Harry said.

He walked to the door. "Come with me, Alberta."

"Wait," Jill said. She thought again. "He can't go with you, because he's a big alligator, and he's stuck under the bed."

"I should have thought of that," Uncle Harry said.

He reached under the bed and began to grunt and groan.

Jill crawled down to the foot of her bed to watch. "What are you doing?" she asked.

"I'm pulling him out," Uncle Harry said.

Suddenly he staggered backward and caught himself against the door. "There! He's not stuck now!"

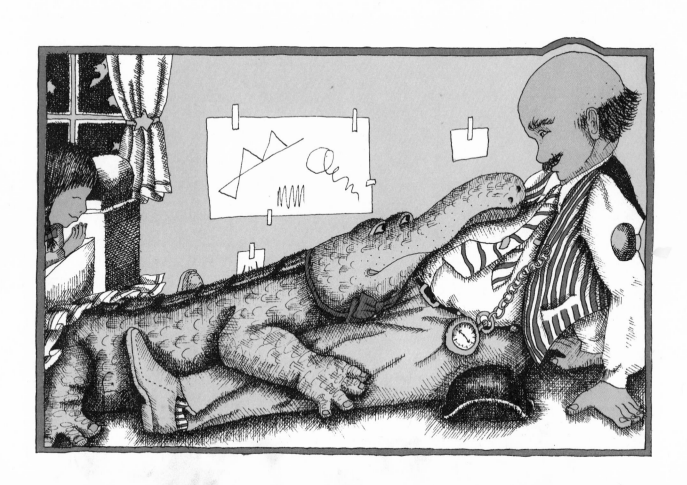

"You got him out?" Jill asked.

"Right," Uncle Harry said. "And now he's going outside and back to his own family. Why don't you stand in the doorway and watch Alberta follow me down the hall?"

Jill jumped out of bed and stood in the doorway. Uncle Harry whistled and snapped his fingers and marched down the hall and around the corner.

Jill scurried down the hall.

She heard the front door open and her father ask, "What are you doing?"

"I'm sending the alligator home," Uncle Harry said.

His voice changed, and he sounded a little cross.

"Good-bye, Alberta," he said. "Don't come back and try those tricks again!"

The front door shut.

"Harry," Jill heard her father say with a laugh, "you and Jill are two of a kind!"

Jill ran back down the hall and jumped into bed. In a few moments she saw Uncle Harry peeking in the doorway.

"Uncle Harry," she asked, "what did Daddy mean when he said we were two of a kind?"

"Hmmmm…maybe he thinks that we look just alike," Uncle Harry said.

Jill giggled, looking at Uncle Harry's mustache and round, fat tummy.

"I know," she said. "I'll bet it was because we knew what to do about Alberta."

"I expect so," Uncle Harry answered. He tucked the blanket around her toes and whispered, "Good night."

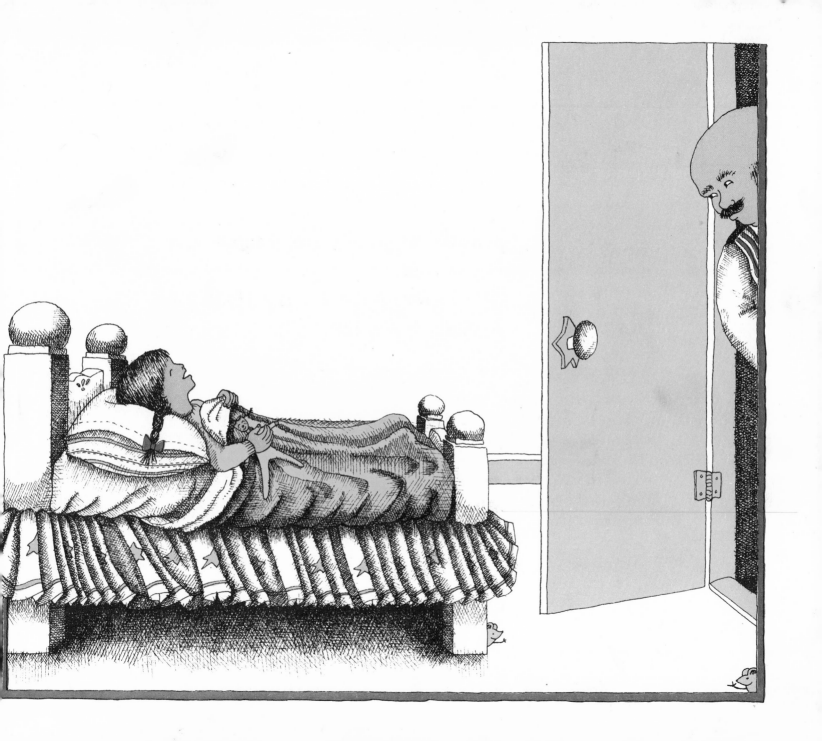

About the Author

JOAN LOWERY NIXON has been a free-lance writer in fiction and nonfiction for twenty-five years. She has written several mystery novels for young readers and an easy-to-read book for children, *The Secret Box Mystery*. Mrs. Nixon and her family live in Midland, Texas.

About the Artist

JAN HUGHES studied at the Moore College of Art in Philadelphia, where she won an award for her use of color in illustration. *The Alligator Under the Bed* is the first book she has illustrated. She has traveled and camped throughout the United States and says she collects anything and everything. Her home is in Hopewell Junction, New York.